Doodles
of Fun!

First published by Parragon in 2013

Parragon
Chartist House
15–17 Trim Street
Bath BA1 1HA, UK
www.parragon.com

Written by Frances Prior-Reeves
Designed by Talking Design
Illustrations by Carol Seatory

ISBN 978-1-4723-1129-0
Printed in China

Doodles of Fun!

PaRragon

Bath · New York · Singapore · Hong Kong · Cologne · Delhi
Melbourne · Amsterdam · Johannesburg · Shenzhen

Fill this window box with

flowers.

Fill this page with
cubes.

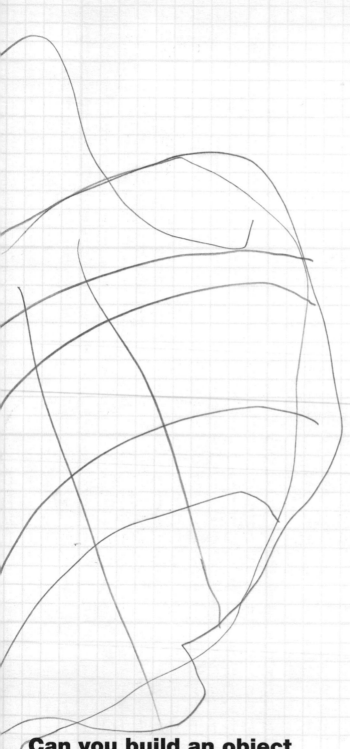

**Can you build an object
from those cubes?**

Design these
bags.

Fill this jar

with candy canes.

Draw the other half of
this owl.

Draw your favorite
animals
in this field all together.

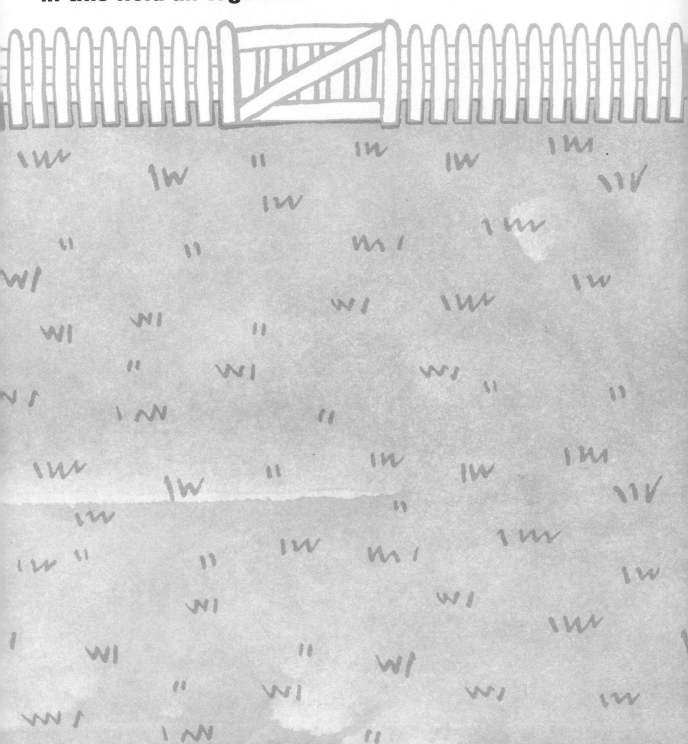

Do they all get along or do you need to draw a divide?

Draw...

a pirate,

a queen,

and a
magician.

Now draw **one**
image of all three.

Color these patterns.

Wrap this gift.

Unwrap

this gift in the space above, what is it?

Decorate
this room for a birthday party.

Draw the

autumn leaves

falling from this tree.

Draw a **playground**
for your parents.

Scribble
in color.

Add some colorful
rain boots
splashing in these puddles.

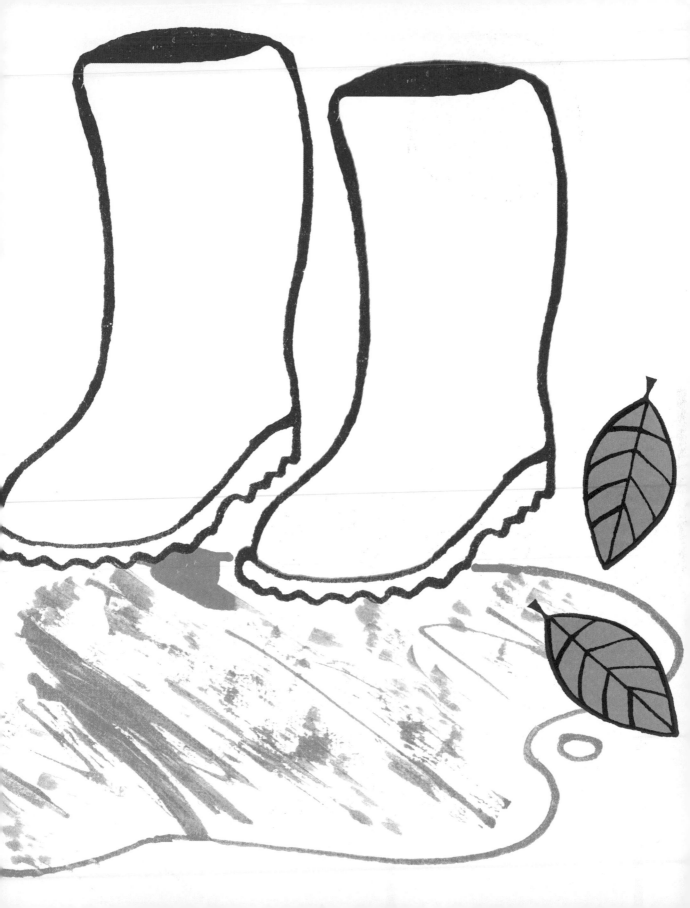

Fill this sky with **kites.**

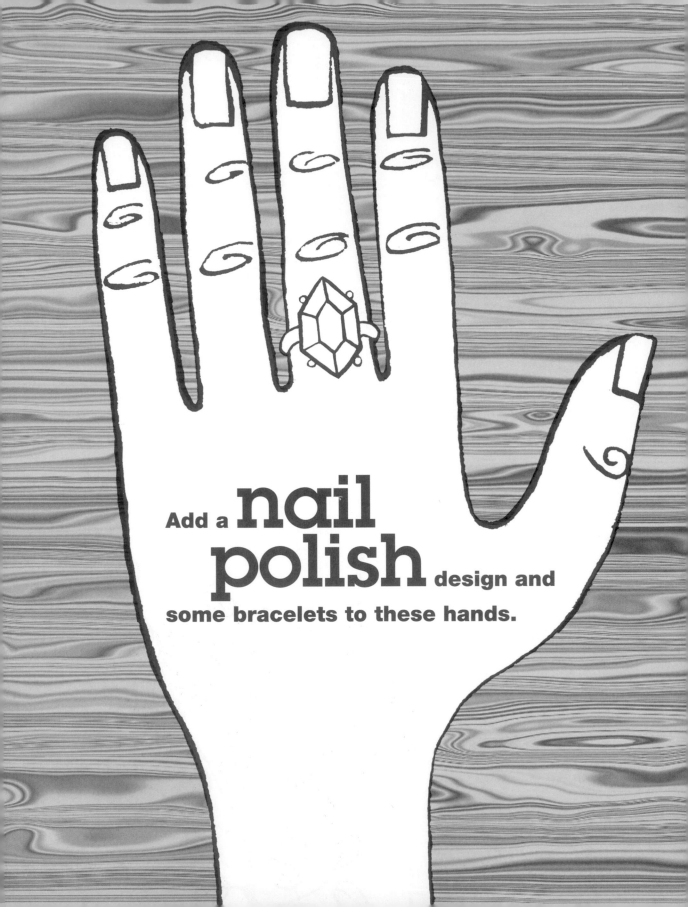

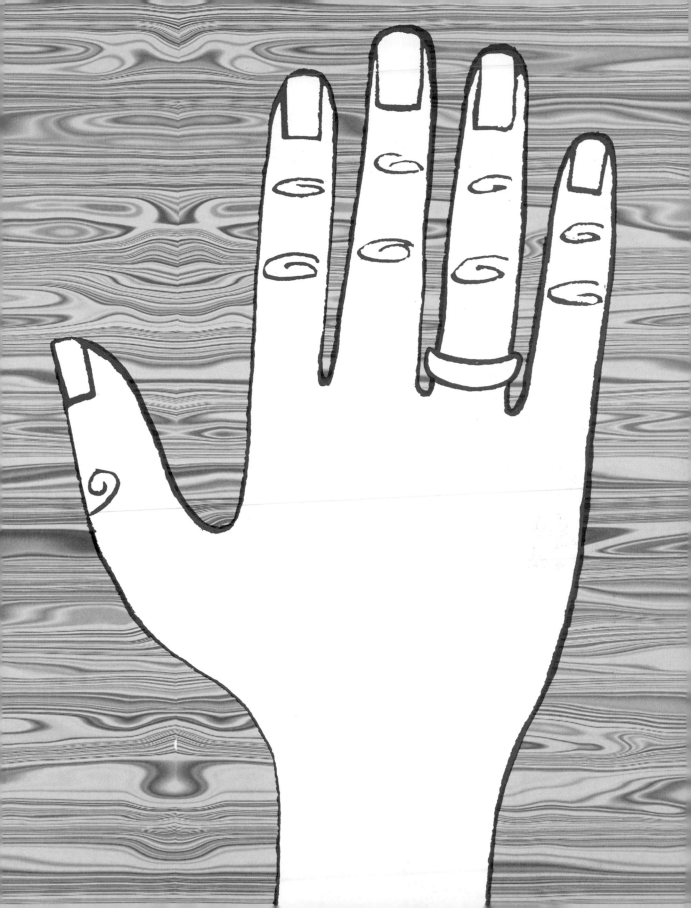

Fill these frames with postmodern **art.**

Draw something you love using only
heart shapes.

Draw an
octopus
having a fight with a
spider.

Draw sandcastles
on this beach.

Draw **yourself**
with your eyes closed.

Draw
yourself
on your head.

Doodle!

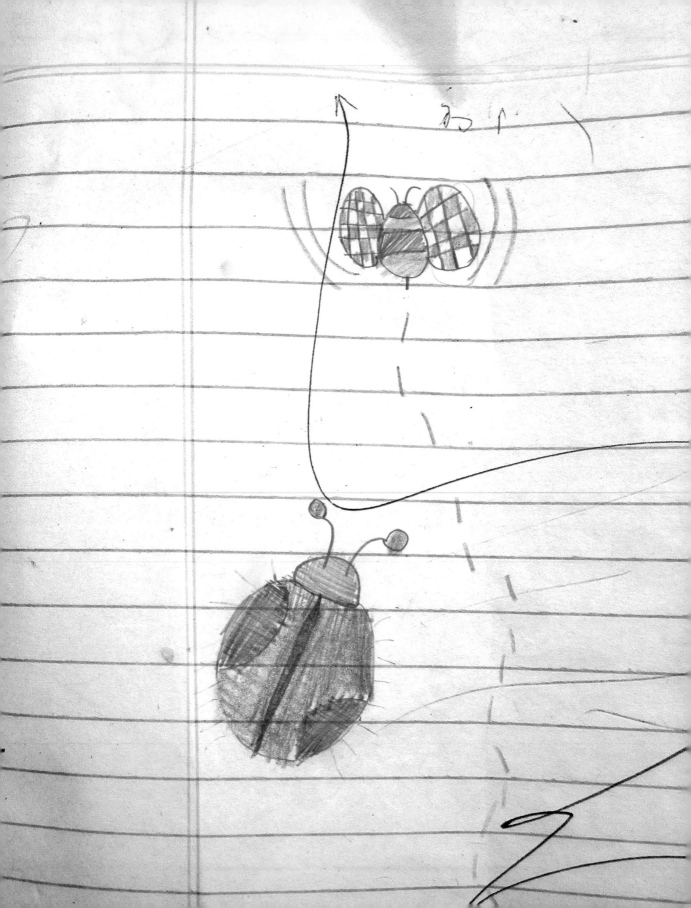

Fill this page with
triangles.

Can you turn those triangles into
butterflies?

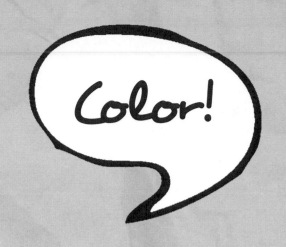

Fill this jar with **keys.**

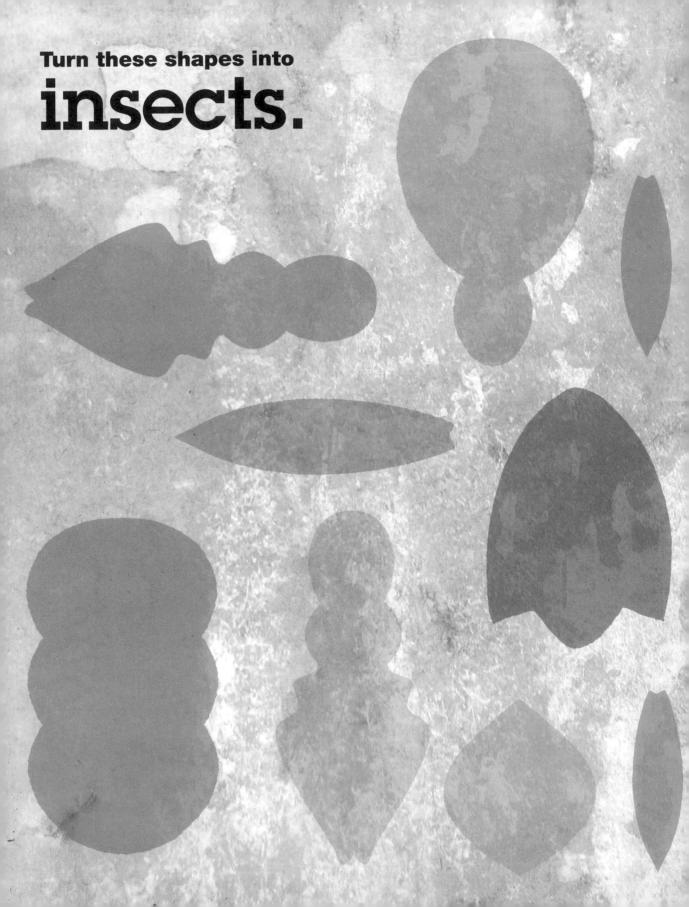

Turn these shapes into
insects.

Draw the other half of this
hot-air
balloon.

Draw some more

passengers ✓

in the basket.

Draw a **galaxy** full of stars.

Create a pattern using
spirals.

Make this house
haunted.

Draw your **favorite thing**
using only your favorite color.

Add ice cream **to these cones.**

Doodle, color, shade, or scribble anything.

Create a colorful pattern
using this graph paper.

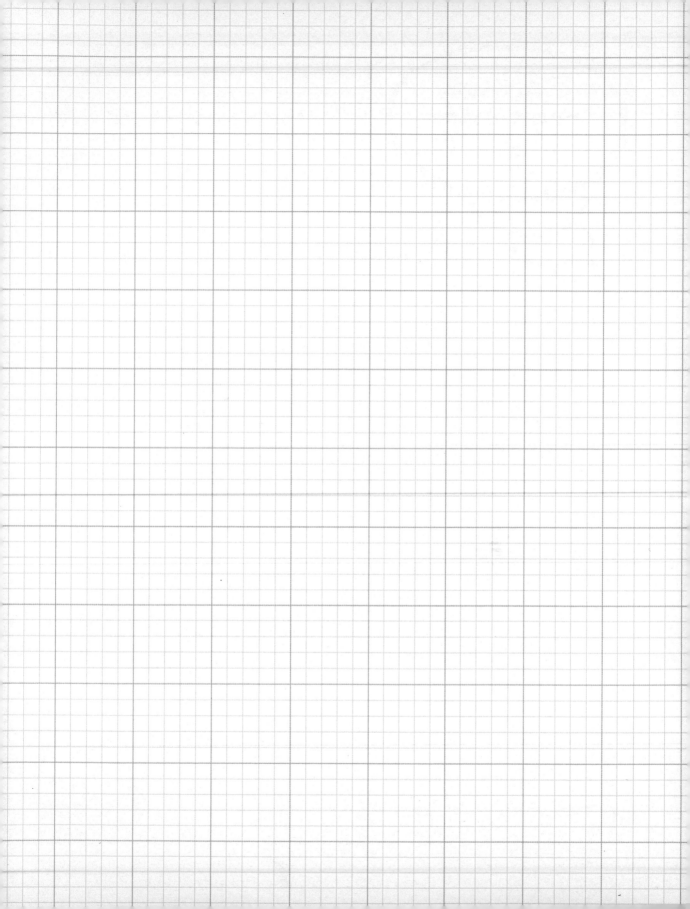

Draw the other half of this
dragon.

Draw some  **people** in line waiting for the sale to start tomorrow.

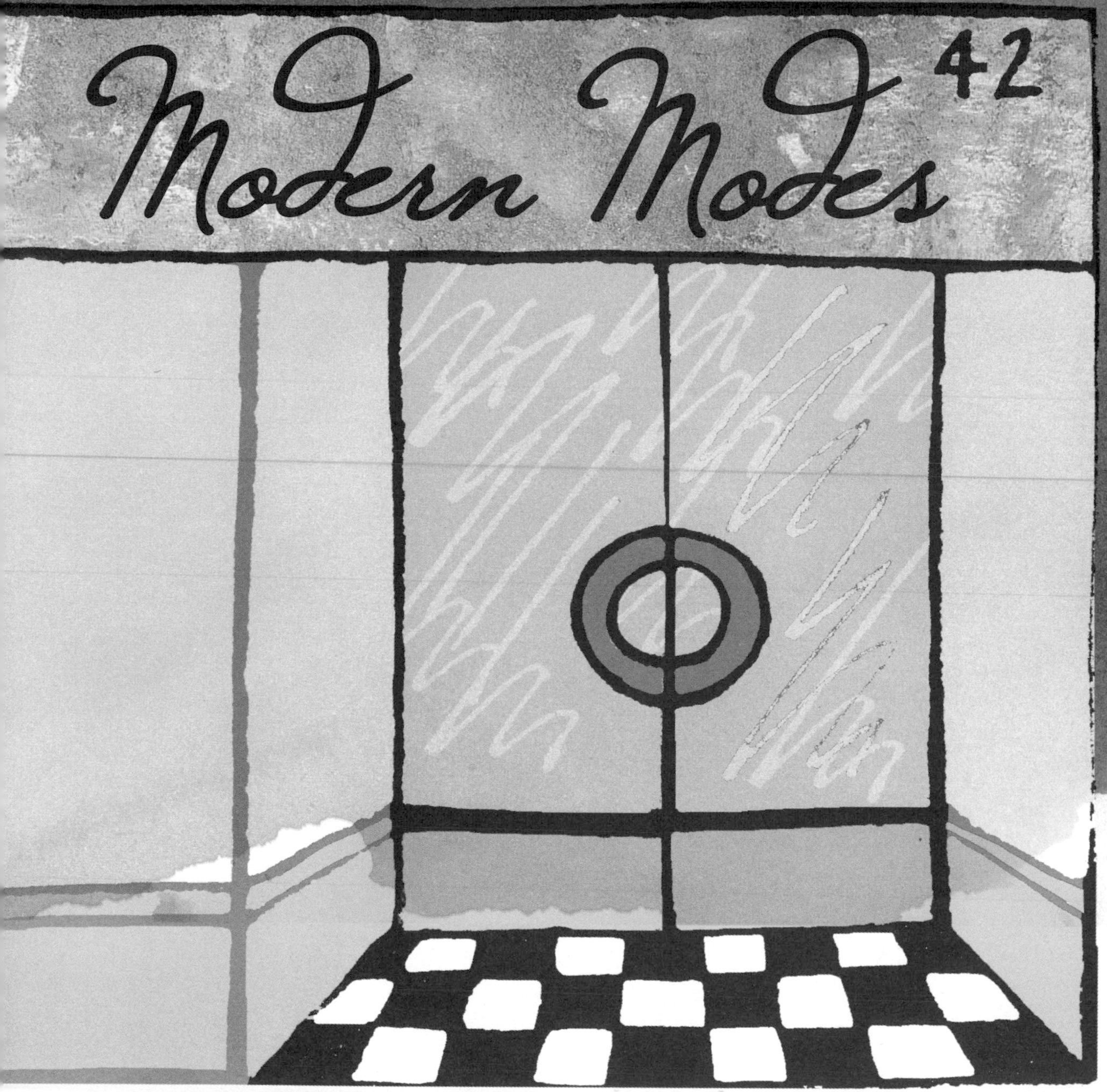
Modern Modes
42

Draw **wings** for yourself and
your best friend and **fly away.**

Draw a **house** using only **circles.**

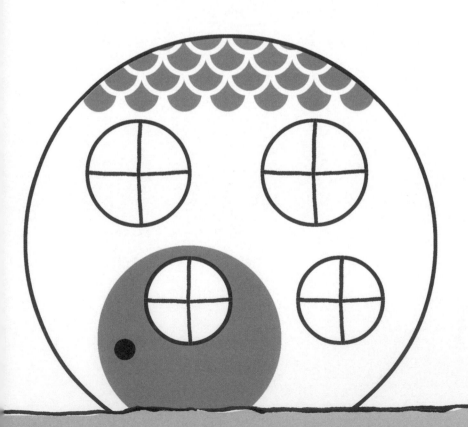

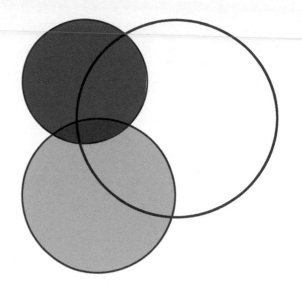

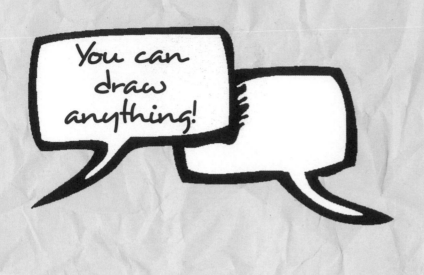

Add **bees** to this beehive.

Plant flowers

for these bees.

Create a **pattern** using only
the letters from your name, over and over.

Grace
Grace
Grdce
Grdc

Fill this **seabed** with things that can **swim.**

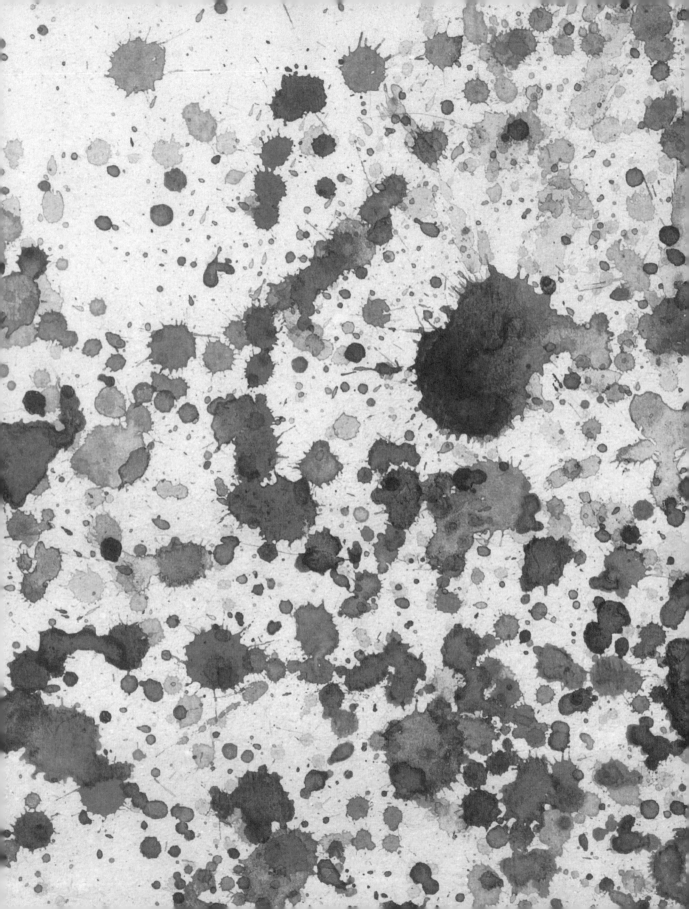

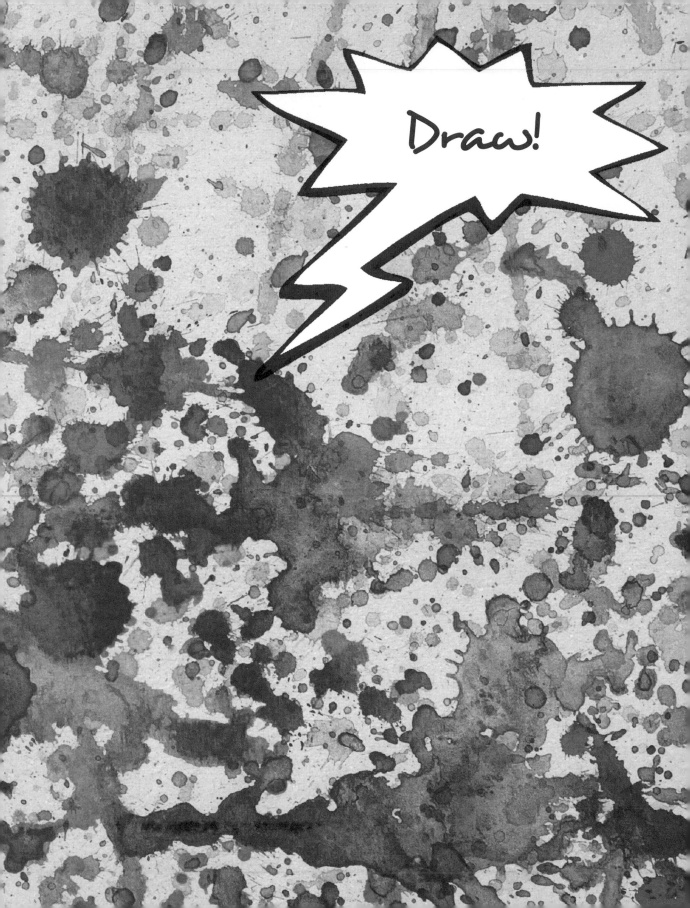

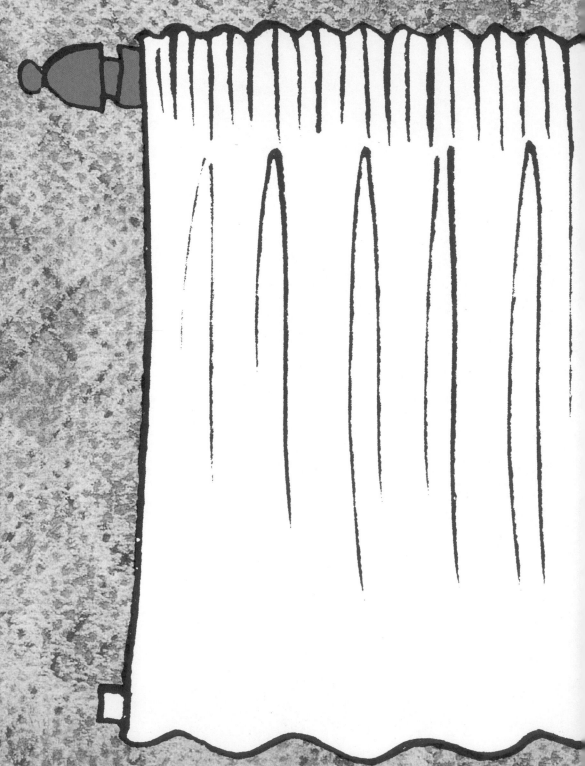

Design these **curtains.**

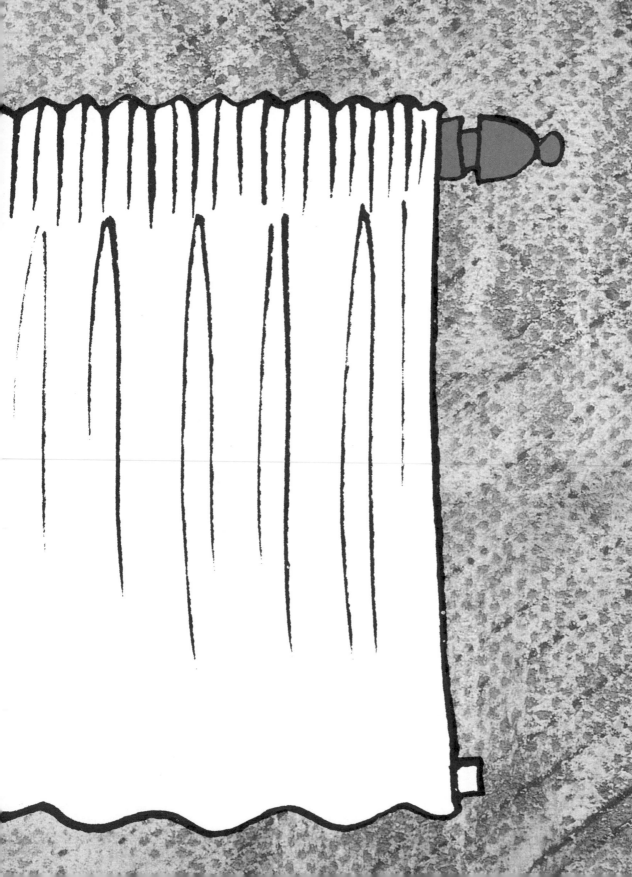

Draw a **bicycle** for this dog.

Color in these **patterns.**

Spread your favorite toppings on these bagels.

Fill this page with animals that come

out in the daytime.

Fill this page with animals that come out at **nighttime.**

Color these
high heels.

Now design your own shoes.

Oodles of doodles!

Draw...

_a donkey,

_a bear,

and a
hippo.

**Now draw one
image of all three.**

Draw an alien spaceship.

Fill this page with
rectangles.

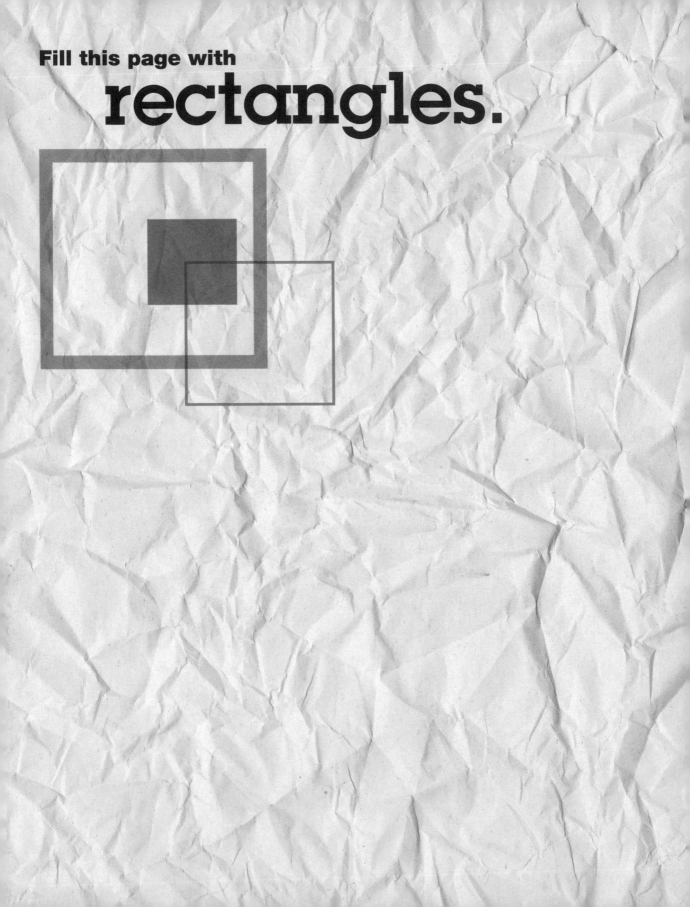

Can you turn those rectangles into a family.

Draw your **story** in this book.

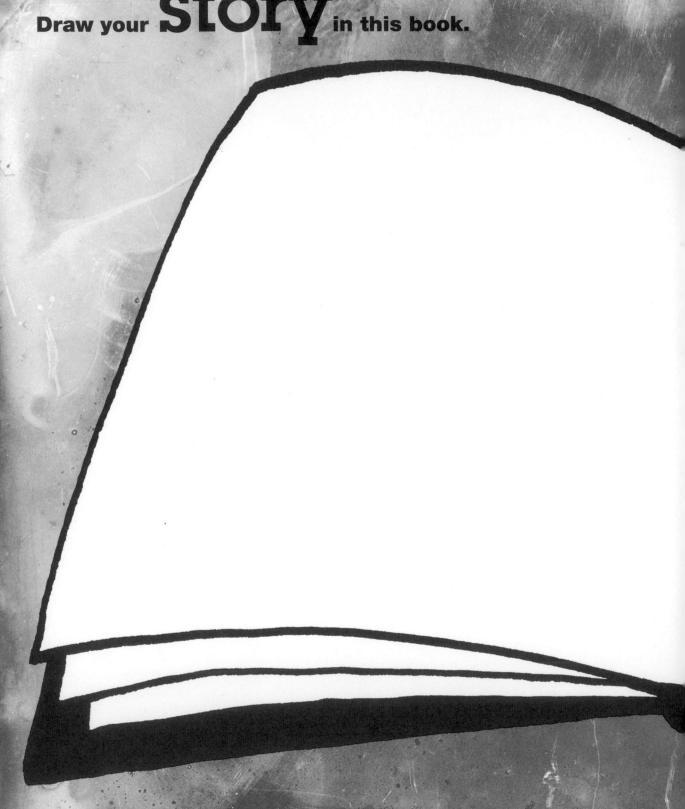

Add dogs

to these collars.

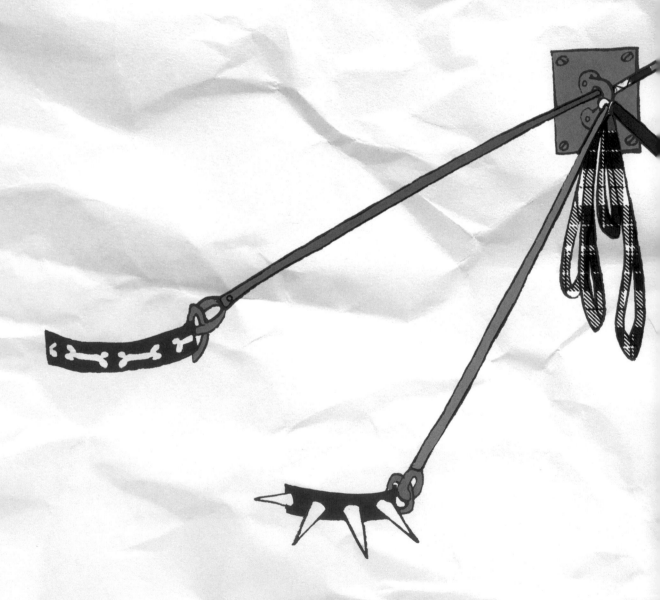

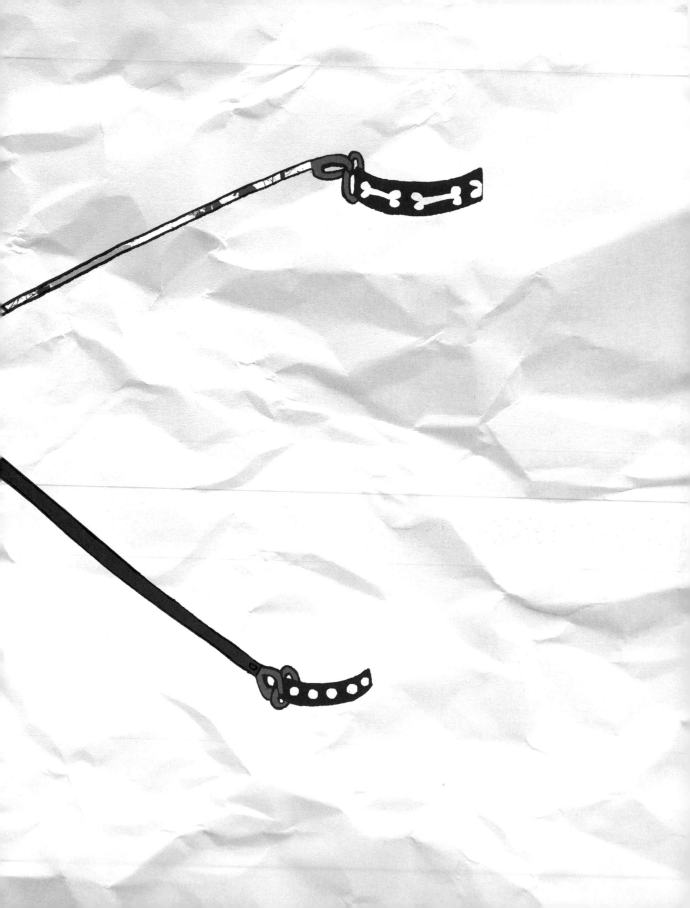

Draw half of
your face
on one side of the circle ...

... and draw half of a
lion's face
on the other side.

Save everything that is
falling.

Color these **hats.**

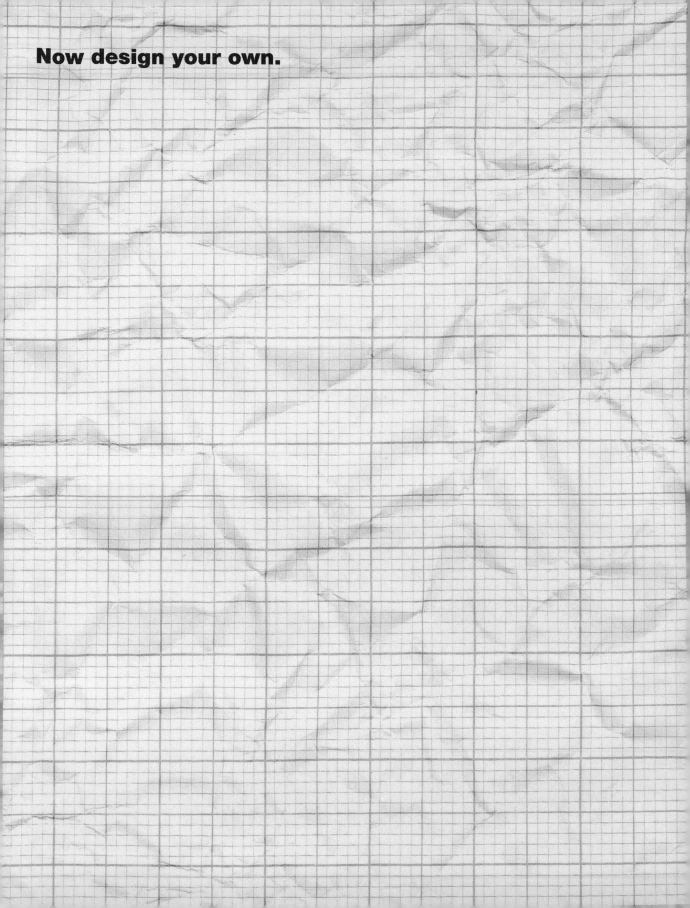

Now design your own.

Fill this sky with things that can fly.

airplanes
butterflies
hot-air balloons

helicopters
fairies dragons
birds

Design the outfit you would wear if you were a
superhero.

Side kick

Design the outfit for your sidekick.

Create!

Fill this row of jars with different size, color, and style

buttons.

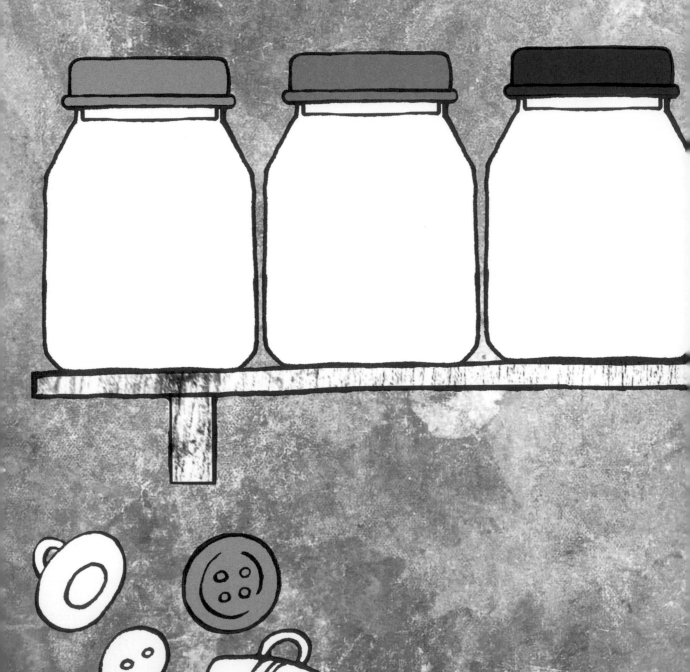

Using this graph paper create a

mosaic.

Create a colorful
pattern.

**For each different color
you use try not taking your
pen from the page.**

Turn this boat into a
pirate ship.

Frost this cake.

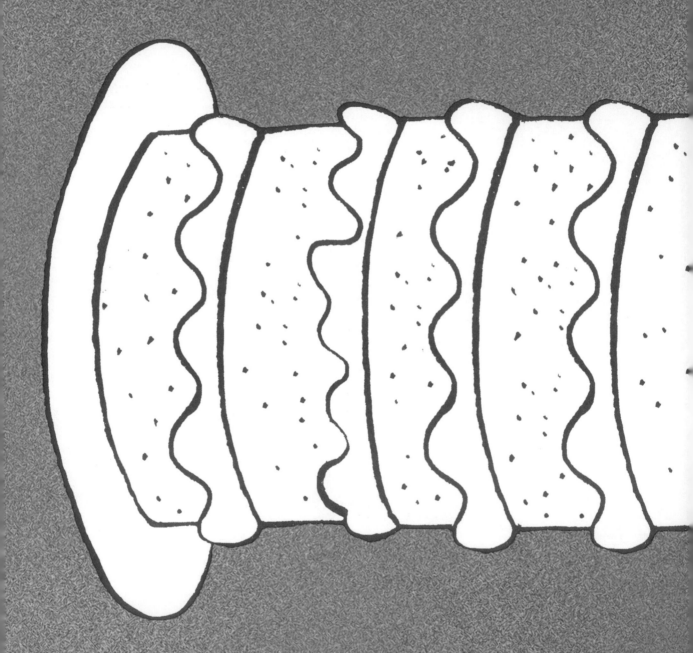

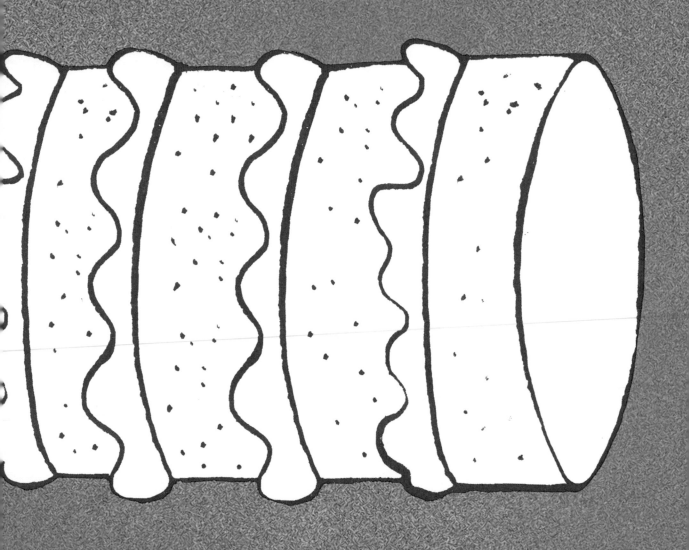

Turn these shapes into monsters.

Fill these pages with
flying pigs.

Draw a
mermaid
on this rock.